One Little Kitten

by
Tana Hoban

SCHOLASTIC BOOK SERVICES
NEW YORK · TORONTO · LONDON · AUCKLAND · SYDNEY · TOKYO

This one is for Max

ISBN 0-590-30894-7

12 11 10 9 8 7 6 5 4 3   0 1 2 3 4 5/8
Printed in the U.S.A.   07

A new day!

A new day!

It's time to play.

A place to hide

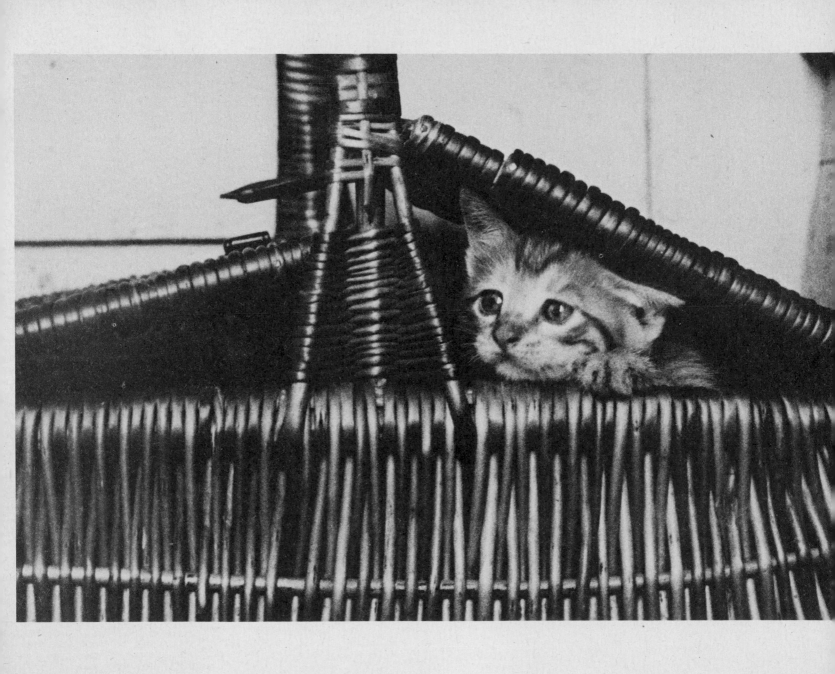

A place to hide

inside.

Where to?

Where to?

Through.

I'll disappear

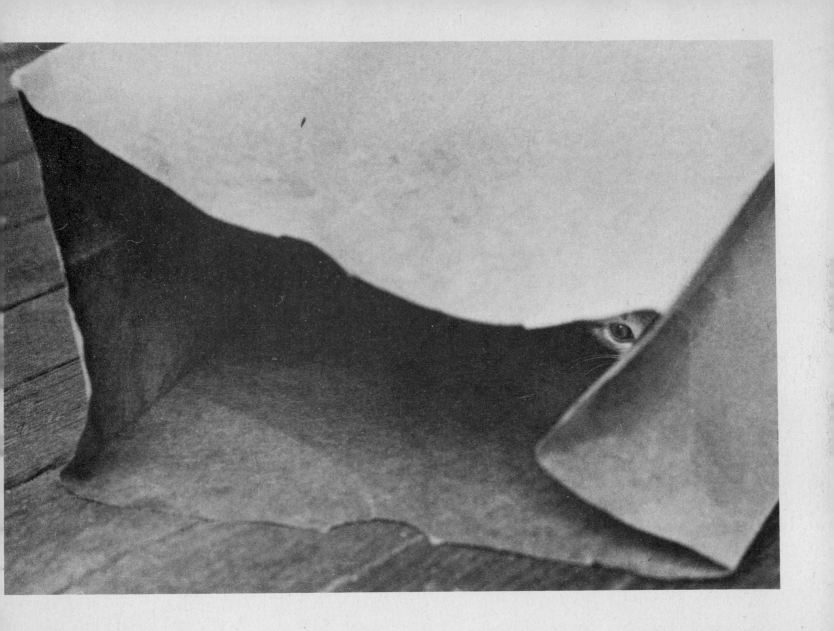

and

come out here.

Is there room?

Is there room

behind this broom?

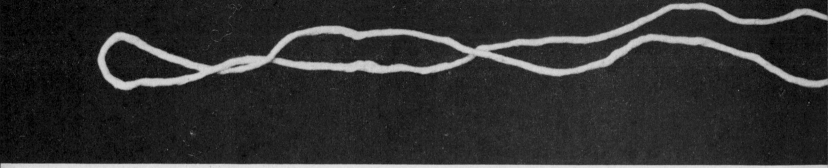

Just the thing–

string!

A funny place

A funny place

to put my face.

It's getting late.

Will they wait?

Hug me tight.

Good night–

Good night.